flowers
for Pudding Street

Christine Mannone Carolan

For Lenny,
Thank you for all the seeds you've sown that make our world a more beautiful place.
Love, CMC

Text and Illustrations copyright © 2009 Christine Mannone Carolan
Inquiries should be addressed to Shenanigan Books, 84 River Road, Summit, New Jersey, 07901.
Library of Congress Cataloging-in-Publication Data

Carolan, Christine.
 Flowers for Pudding Street / written and illustrated by Christine Mannone Carolan.
   p. cm.
 Summary: When Miss Violet from the garden club presents the residents of Pudding Street with a special award for
prettiest flowers, no one--except for a clever dog and a busy bird--knows who has been doing all the planting.
 ISBN 978-1-934860-02-1
 [1. Gardening--Fiction. 2. Flowers--Fiction. 3. Neighborhoods--Fiction. 4. Dogs--Fiction. 5. Birds--Fiction.] I. Title.
 PZ7.C2189Fl 2009
 [E]--dc22

                            2009031282

Printed in China
first edition 1 October 2009
This product conforms to CPSIA 2008

A Note from the Author & Friends

Did you ever see flowers and trees in the wild and wonder who planted them? People love to plant seeds and watch them grow, but seeds don't always get started this way. Most of them are planted the way they were millions of years ago – before there were people on earth.

Sometimes seeds are carried by the wind and grow where they land. Sometimes they float on the water and wash up on new shores. Other times, they attach themselves to the fur of animals and ride to their new homes. In some cases, squirrels bury them on the floor of a forest, or birds drop them in your backyard.

We have only to look around us to see the fascinating ways that nature spreads seeds – including some where humans lend a hand. Have you ever noticed a seed taking a piggyback ride in your hair, or on your clothes, or in your shoe? Have you ever picked a dandelion and blown its tiny seed parachutes into the wind?

No wonder the earth is covered with beautiful forests and fields and meadows!
No wonder there are flowers on Pudding Street – and on your street and mine!

This morning, Miss Violet
from the garden club
presented Pudding Street
with a special award
for the prettiest flowers in town.

I remember the day I noticed
the first flower growing.
It was a sunflower taller than me!

Every day after that,
more and more sunflowers grew
and everyone wondered
who was planting them.
Even I didn't know at first.

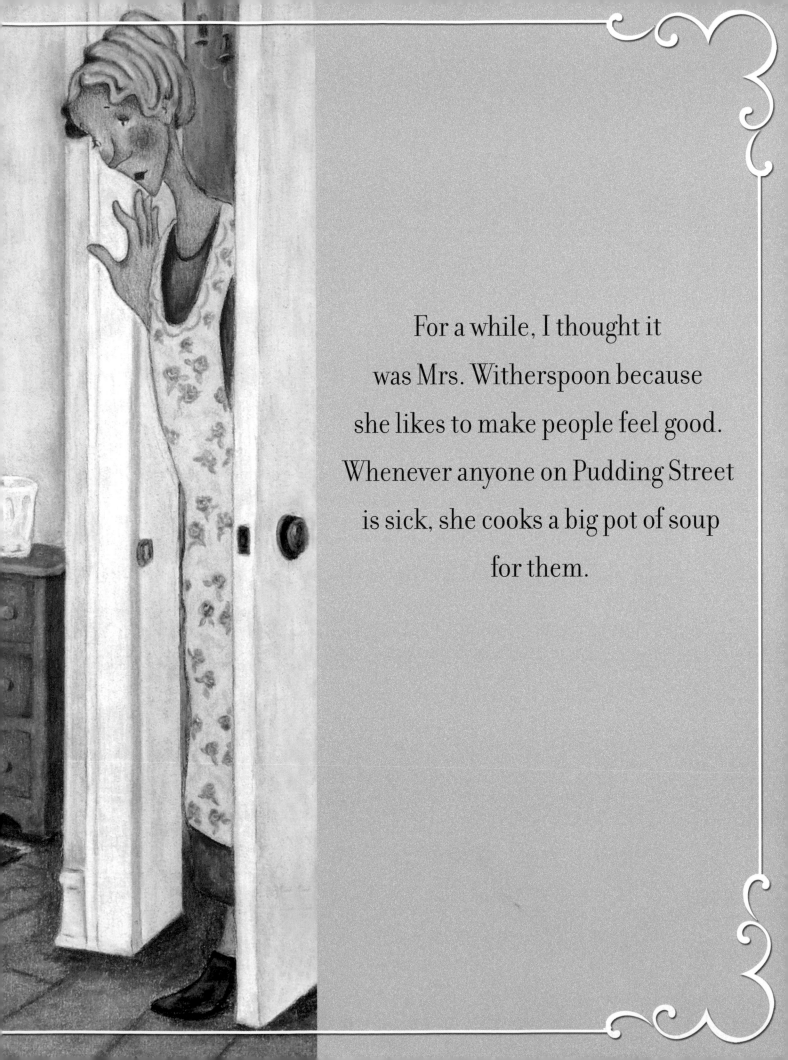

For a while, I thought it
was Mrs. Witherspoon because
she likes to make people feel good.
Whenever anyone on Pudding Street
is sick, she cooks a big pot of soup
for them.

Next, I thought it was Mr. Crowley who feeds the birds. After all…he has bags of sunflower seeds.

Then I imagined it was friendly Mr. Merola.
He always takes the time to do something
special for others.

People watched very closely,
and every day more and more flowers popped up!
But who was planting them?

Was it Miss Crumpet?

She likes to make things look pretty.

Could it be Tommy?
He rides up and down
Pudding Street every day.

Perhaps it was Miss Bean.
Everyone on Pudding Street says
she has a green thumb.

Was it Daisy and Fern?

They love flowers.

Nobody knew who was planting the flowers,
but everyone was talking about it
and trying to guess who it was.

So today, everyone waited
anxiously to see who
would accept the award
from Miss Violet,
but when she presented the ribbon,
no one came forward.

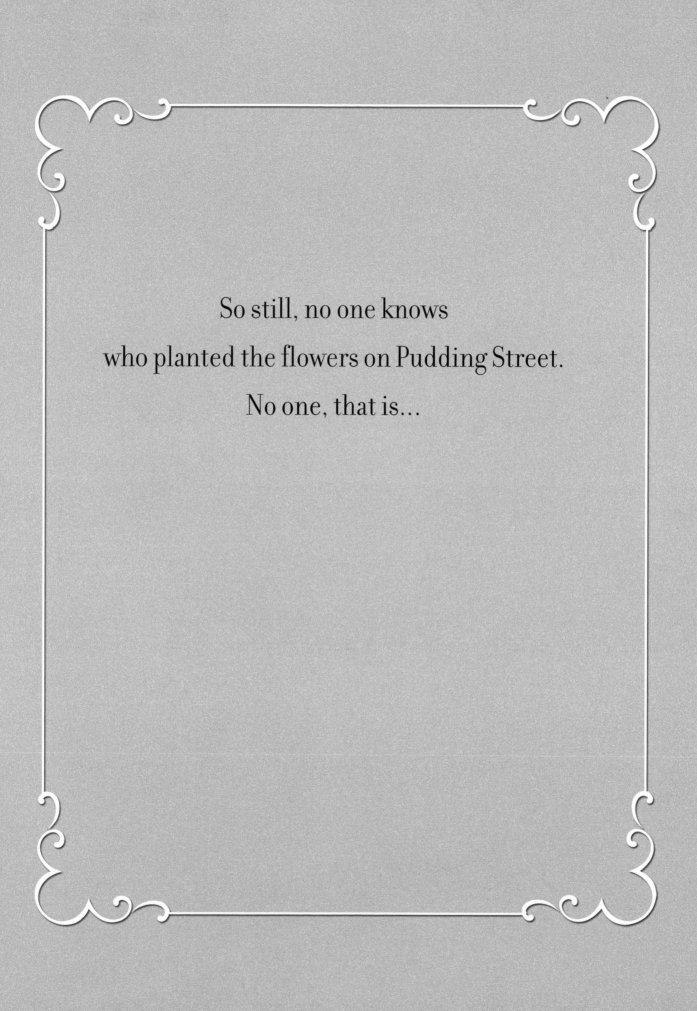

So still, no one knows

who planted the flowers on Pudding Street.

No one, that is…

except us.